# WHERE IT ENDS

A Novella-in-Flash

Heather Walker

Copyright © 2021 Heather Walker

All rights reserved

The characters and events portrayed in this book are fictitious. Any similarity to real persons, living or dead, is coincidental and not intended by the author.

No part of this book may be reproduced, or stored in a retrieval system, or transmitted in any form or by any means, electronic, mechanical, photocopying, recording, or otherwise, without express written permission of the publisher.

ISBN: 9798491156658

Cover design by: Art Painter
Library of Congress Control Number: 2018675309
Printed in the United States of America

*To Diane*

# CONTENTS

Title Page
Copyright
Dedication
Where It ends
December — 1
Escapade — 2
Ambush — 4
Lawrence — 6
Harry — 8
Sara — 9
Unearthing — 11
Where it ends — 13
Enoch — 14
Mary — 16
The Language of Trees — 18
Feet — 19
Space – the final frontier — 21
Dignity — 23
Arthur — 25
Radiation — 27
Sixth Sense — 28

| | |
|---|---|
| The Wrong Man | 29 |
| River Rising | 31 |
| Acknowledgement | 33 |
| About The Author | 35 |
| Afterword | 37 |

# WHERE IT ENDS

# DECEMBER

December creeps in on heavy clouds that threaten rain. Dampness is a cloak that smothers all. The oak weeps with its cousins and old stones prepare to weather another winter.

In the chapel, where the Book of Remembrance is kept, a small Christmas tree has been placed close to the door. Are its bright lights a comfort or hindrance to those who come here? Not for the dead, obviously, but for the living who will have one less place to lay for on Christmas Day. They don't need a reminder of who won't be there.

Outside, the drive is busy with black hearses coming and going. Black suited men, women in black wool coats, hover in the damp wishing and not wishing it was over. Small children wait to be told what to do, where to go, and not entirely understanding why. But does anyone know the answers to what is happening today?

Bright flowers come in wreaths and cellophane, swathes of colour on an otherwise dull day. Cold clings to the mourners like a wet winding sheet. It is a day to be got through however one can.

Daylight fades before it's even got going and by four-thirty the gates are closed and locked. Only the dead are free to roam here now as night bears down.

# ESCAPADE

Bailey and Jack. Two peas in a pod. Always together. Always into mischief. Tonight, they meet at Burger King, stuff themselves with double cheeseburgers and strawberry milkshakes and set off along Bridgeforth Road towards the cemetery fired up for their latest escapade.

The gates close at four-thirty in winter, but they are not sure when the office closes, so they aim to get there around six-thirty. There is a moon which is all to the good, but now they have to climb over the gates. Bailey gives Jack a leg up and he scrambles higher on the frosted bars, fingers icing as he goes. At twelve, the boys are small for their age, but they are fast and agile.

Once over, Bailey turns his mobile to record. The two boys push into one another so they are both in shot.

'Here we are in the cemetery with the dead,' says Bailey. Jack giggles. 'It's dark and eerie. Will we see any ghosts?' Bailey emphasises the 's', snakelike.

The boys walk the pathways with Jack using the torch on his mobile to guide them. Everything looks different in the dark. Something swoops overhead. 'Shit, what was that?' Jack says.

'Just an owl,' Bailey says. 'There'll be all sorts of creatures out at this time.' Bailey presses record again.

'Isn't the light too low?' Jack asks.

'It's fine, Jack. Stop worrying.'

They explore the tombs, the winged angel on top of Frederick Mathews' grave. Reading the descriptions, there is a whole host of family bodies buried below. 'I think I'd rather burn,' Bailey says.

'But can you still haunt if you are cremated? I want to haunt a whole lot of people. I mean is there even an afterlife if you go up in smoke?'

'Yes, you wazzock. Your soul leaves your body before it's disposed of. Did no one tell you that?'

Bailey presses stop on the video. 'I got something tonight. Nicked it off my brother.' He pulls a tin from the pocket of his puffer jacket and opens the lid. 'Weed.'

They find a headstone to sit against and light up the smokes. They take in a lungful, cough and giggle.

'Warms you up, eh?' Bailey says.

Once they start giggling, they can't stop until two bright eyes shine before them. 'Fuckin' 'ell,' they say together. The eyes move and a shape darts to the right.

'A fox. It's a fox, Jack,' and they begin giggling all over again.

They stagger up, walk towards the new arrivals. Some hadn't yet got headstones. They look along the row and then Jack stops. 'That's my name, my date of birth.' He leans forward. 'Jesus, Bailey, the future yet to come,' Jack howls. 'Fuck, fuck,' and he starts running. Bailey can't see anything written on the headstone. His eyes are all blurry, but he follows Jack. They've done what they set out to do at least.

# AMBUSH

He sees her across the cemetery. She doesn't appear to be weeping today. Joe remembers the weight of her head on his shoulder.

Joe waits. There isn't much to do this time of year, but after the snow he is clearing paths and salting them. The sun makes the snow glisten in a pretty way.

He goes to the standpipe next to the grave she is bent over. 'Hello,' he says. She looks up and smiles bashfully. 'Cold day.' She smiles again. 'Why don't you come into the chapel for a bit and get warm.'

She stands, and without a word follows him along the uncleared path. Inside the chapel, warm air wafts and she lifts her head as if to bathe in it. Joe closes the door.

'Why don't you take your coat off, or you won't feel the benefit of it when you go back out.'

'That's something mother would say.' She says it blandly, but begins to undo the buttons and shrugs it off. Joe helps and lays it on the back of a pew. She stares at the stained-glass window where the sun casts coloured rays across the chapel.

Joe knows her sadness for she told him. She still lives at home. Her mother is manipulative and uses emotional blackmail to keep her there. She is weak, thinks Joe, and vulnerable, especially with her father gone. She blames him for leaving her with her mother. She told Joe that when she wept on his shoulder.

Joe moves the stone doorstop in front of the doors as a temporary lock. She isn't pretty. She could make more of herself with a decent hairstyle, and clothes that fitted. He turns to her. She's nervy, but stares into his eyes. Joe leans forward and covers her mouth with his. She pulls back. Joe's hand pushes her head towards him, bruising their lips. He feels her hand grip his arm, hears a small noise in her throat. Then his hand is on her breast. She gasps. Joe's hand slides down to the hem of her sweater, up and under it until he feels her nipple through her blouse. She jumps, squirms, while Joe's other hand squeezes her buttocks, clasping her tight to him, to his hardness. She tries to push away.

Joe's hand leaves the nipple and slides down to find the waistband of her trousers. This time she wrenches away just as the door rattles. They stand apart, her face is white and scared. She grabs her coat and makes for the door, but it will not open. Joe comes over, kicks the stone away and the door is rent backwards. A woman in a furry hat pushes in as the girl slips through and out.

'I thought the chapel was locked,' the woman says. Joe doesn't answer. He races out of the door to see the girl walking quickly away to the gates. She won't tell, he thinks. Anyway, she didn't object. She never said no. Not really.

# LAWRENCE

She stood by the back door, spring sunshine warming her. The first time she had felt any warmth that day. Behind her the children were noisy, a babbling of voices drummed into her head. She stepped into the garden to find some peace. The tulips were already turning, lilac was blossoming against the wall and the vegetable beds were dug ready for planting.

Alison sits on the low wall and wonders why it all still goes on. If she'd had her way, she would have gone with him. Immediately she feels guilty. She has Rick and the girls. They need her, but she wishes they didn't.

Why did she have to be the adult today? To supervise the outfits, the buffet, who stood where, sat where, make sure everything ran as it should. All she wanted to do was be with Lawrence one last time.

He was her everything. After the death of their parents he had been her rock. They'd gone to live with an aunt, her father's sister. Life had been different but okay, Lawrence had seen to that. And now he was gone. Alison leans forward, pain ripping into her. She had never thought she'd have to arrange a funeral for her brother, at least not until they were both old. It was so unfair!

Lawrence had never married. He'd never seemed that interested in girls. He liked to have his hands in the earth, to cultivate the soil and grow things. These vegetable beds were his doing. Now they mocked her.

At the crematorium she had watched Lawrence's coffin move slowly along what she called the supermarket conveyer belt. Where it was going, she could not. The curtains closing was so final. Alison felt her life closing.

For a moment this morning she had woken bright, and then that awful heaviness fell on her as she remembered he'd gone. And it was so fast. A freak accident on his motorbike, a skid off the road and into a tree. Her beautiful brother gone in the click of the fingers.

She had made sure there were masses of flowers today. He'd have liked that. And she had brought some home thinking it would bring some comfort, but the empty hole was too deep to fill. Alison's sudden cry frightened a flock of pigeons busy on the lawn. She wanted to be with Lawrence wherever he was. She couldn't go on alone.

She felt a hand on her shoulder and jumped. Lawrence's name was on her lips, but it was Rick. She leaned into his arm and sobbed. He sat down beside her and encircled her against his chest. He didn't say a word. He didn't have to. He wasn't Lawrence. He would never be Lawrence, but he would do. She clung to him as music spilled out from the house. Someone was playing Lawrence's favourite song.

# HARRY

The bench is warm, the wood giving back what it has received. Harry's body moulds into it as he tucks into his sandwich. Banana and peanut butter today. His favourite. From his vantage point, the top of the steep side of the cemetery, he watches the pall bearers raise the coffin on to their shoulders. Later, Harry will seek out the spot and pay his respect. He always does that. He feels it is part of his job, though there was nothing about it in the job description when he signed his contract. Still, it's the right thing to do.

It is a small affair. Only a handful of mourners today. Harry wonders what that says about the departed. Are they a dearly departed or something else? Of course, he's seen it all over the years. Crowds milling around as if it's a party, shaking hands, air kissing, dressed in their Sunday best, or hovering awkwardly, unsure of what to do, how they will see it through and meet that awkward relative no one likes. There are the graveside wailings, the flowers and soil caught in the wind as they are scattered over the coffin six feet down.

So much black at these funerals. So depressing. That's not the way he wants it. He wants all the colours of life, and he wants to rest here with those he has come to know in these last ten years.

Harry pours tea from his flask and listens to the sparrows fighting in the bush behind him. He loves to hear their chatter as he sips his tea. Afterwards he packs away his lunch and stands. He wipes his napkin over the brass plate on the back of the bench and thanks Mabel for her company today. Then he makes his way back to the office by the cemetery entrance. There will be new names to go in the book, new people to visit during his lunch hours.

# SARA

It is that time of year when thick coats are shed. Everyone feels lighter. Even here, life is beginning again, turning its face away from the dark days of winter, bringing colour to where the dead sleep. Crocus shoot up between the graves and the garden of remembrance holds a promise of renewal.

Sara holds a bunch of wild flowers in her hand as she walks through the cold flower room, reading cards loved ones have left. She admires every photo, poem and memento people have brought. She considers her friends to be here, among the flower heads arranged in tall metal and glass vases tiered against the walls. She has come to know who is who, sees new offerings arrive for them monthly.

Sara draws in a long breath of flowery scent, fills her lungs with it. She fingers a rose petal, red and velvety, and sighs knowing it is almost time she left.

Some months ago, she came here on a whim, for some peace and quiet, to get away from a world that misunderstood her, a world where she felt she no longer belonged. Among the flowers and gravestones Sara found acceptance.

Coming into the flower room felt like an intrusion at first. Sara had no relatives laid to rest here or any that needed remembering, yet all those names and photos drew her back time and time again. The longing to stay was overwhelming, to not have to worry about anything ever again. She wondered who would come and visit her, remember her. Maybe that nice man from the office who smiles at her when they see each other. She likes his manner, the way he touches the headstones, runs a hand over name plates.

She places a wild flower in each vase as she passes, until the flowers run out. Sara walks into the sunshine. Her eyes scan the cemetery but she cannot see the man from the office. At the gates she pauses. Next time they meet she will be brave and ask him his name.

# UNEARTHING

A river flows on the north side of town, winding its way down past the cemetery. In nineteen forty-eight the river burst its banks and flooded the oldest part of the graveyard. Gravestones collapsed and there were horror stories of bodies floating, becoming caught on the bars of the railings, their bloated remains bursting.

Adam Kent heard these stories and came to explore for himself, though it was fifteen years after the event. He booked into *The Swan* and spent hours at the cemetery, the public library and interviewing town's people about the flood. Some stories were second hand, or from friends of friends, but they were all blood curdling. The pub became his interview space. People bought him drinks and he bought them in return.

Agnes Draper said her late husband (thankfully not that late – his body was well and truly in the ground) had taken photos. She promised to unearth them. It was 'unearth' that made Adam giggle, though that might have had something to do with the four pints of bitter. Unearthing became Adam's watchword. It seemed everyone had a story to tell, though how many of them were true was hard to say. Only Adam's visit to the library kept him sane. At least the local history publications seemed authentic, but slivers of skin wrapped around railings and stretched between tombstones? Adam took that with a pinch of salt.

The unearthing of the Agnes' photos took several days and Adam was running out of time and money on this project. He needed to go home and write everything up properly. His notes were often scribbles, undecipherable gibberish. And the photos? It was difficult to tell what was what.

'That there is a head,' Agnes said proudly. 'Just washed away. God knows where the body went.'

Adam stared at the photo. There was far too much black in the black and white photo and it was so small, but wasn't that part of an elaborate tomb, rather than a real head? He made the mistake of saying so to Agnes, who promptly scooped up all the photos and put them in her handbag.

'Well, if that's your attitude.' Agnes stood up bumping ample hips against the small round table. The half empty glasses shook.

Adam apologised, but it was too late. Agnes was gone. Adam finished his beer and stood up. He swayed slightly as he headed outside and down to the cemetery. The night was blacker than black. No moon to cast its light across the headstones. The gates were shut and Adam leaned on the railings feeling slightly queasy. A shriek turned his blood cold. A sweep of air overhead startled him. Through the railings it went, a trail of mist following. The being turned and smiled at him. Adam bolted, falling over his feet. He ran back to *The Swan*. The next day he paid his bill and left. He never came back, and if the book was written, it never graced a book shelf.

# WHERE IT ENDS

Mist floats in ethereal clouds - in, out and around the gravestones. Tree limbs stand muted against stone and marble. At this hour, before the sun rises, before the day really begins, you could imagine the bones of the dead gathering together one last time to exchange lives, swap stories about family and how it ended. They might greet the newcomers, admire their flowers, read with them the messages of their loved ones and wonder how words were used that were never spoken in life, never expressed by a hug or a kiss, yet now they are described as sorely missed.

They may seep through the walls of the chapel, scan the Book of Remembrance to find their name, just to make sure what had happened was real. And some may meet with their departed family – a husband, wife, parents, long lost relatives they had never met before.

And now the mist is parting. A ray of yellow casts a shadow across this place. The bones return, recent ashes swirl and settle. If they are lucky someone will come today. Maybe talk to them, lay a flower or two, and they will rest knowing they are remembered. They will feel reassured that they are not just a name in a book, a body boxed, burned or buried.

# ENOCH

On the other side of the river is the cottage where Enoch lives. Enoch doesn't know how he came by that name. His mother wasn't religious and it wasn't a name that had been passed down through the family. At school he was bullied about it, 'Ee-noch on that door!' the cry often came, but Enoch just got on with it. That was his philosophy in life, and really what other way was there?

He'd got on with it when he'd left school and ended up in the chicken factory. His mother had kept chickens and some Sundays she would go wring the neck of one for dinner. Enoch never thought anything about it. But in the factory, he'd never seen so many half-bald and sick birds. This was not a place anyone would want to meet their end. Some chickens still quivered as they met the scald bath to strip off what feathers they had left. A condemned man going to the noose wouldn't be treated like that. It wasn't right.

Enoch got on with it when his wife died. He had to because he was left with Archie and he was only ten. He got on with it when Archie was arrested and sent to Young Offenders. Fingers pointed at him. People stopped conversations when he entered a shop, but he just got on with it and visited Archie when he could.

He got on with it when he lost his job. The chicken factory was re-locating too far for him to travel. In one way it was a relief, but in another he had no idea what he would do. Now he worked as a street cleaner. Out in all weathers and despite the heat and the cold, it was better than the noise and death of the chicken factory.

Life went on. Archie returned, only to end up in adult prison a year later after an armed robbery in a jewellery shop. Sometimes, it seemed to Enoch that he was constantly sweeping up parts of himself along the pavements and gutters. But there was no point in thinking on it. Best just get on with it.

But last week he had the results back from the tests and it was the worst news. Dying was going to happen whatever he did, so it was best to get on with it.

Enoch crossed the river by the little bridge down near the lock and went to the cemetery. He went there often to see his Mildred. Today he went to tell her the news. He'd never told her about Archie's troubles. It would have upset her too much. She'll know soon enough when we meet again, Enoch thought.

On his return, Enoch arranged a visit to Archie. He had to prepare him, make things right. Everything would go to him anyway. He just hoped his son would be careful. He wrote the instructions for a simple funeral and then Enoch got on with living.

# MARY

Mary visits Alex daily. She brings with her a fold-up garden chair because she knows she's going to be a long time. She often brings tea and biscuits as well.

When he was alive Alex was in charge of everything. He decided when rooms needed decorating and what colour, the layout and planting of the garden, where they would holiday and how the children should be brought up. And talk. Boy could he talk. Their son was just the same and Mary was overwhelmed by the noise, and there was never a large enough gap for her to say anything. Their daughter left home not long after leaving school. 'There are too many words in this house,' she said, but what could Mary do? When their son left there was just her and Alex, and once Alex retired, her ears rang with his voice. There was no respite. At church he was a reader (of course) and sometimes helped with communion. He took over the conversation after the service as they drank coffee, and he had an opinion on everything. His favourite expression was, 'Oh, Mary doesn't have an opinion on that.' Of course, she did, but he never asked her, and if she had managed to get a word in, he'd not have listened. He had a way of talking over her as soon as she opened her mouth.

Her only escape was the WI, where she felt supported and listened to. But even then, Alex complained about evening meetings because they 'went on a bit' and he wanted to lock up for the night.

The first thing Mary noticed after Alex died was the quiet. She could breathe. She could hear her own thoughts, and she realised she could do anything she liked. So, she called a decorator in and changed the bland magnolia lounge walls for a rich burgundy feature wall contrasted with sherbet lemon. She threw wild flower seeds into the flowerbeds and left the dandelions alone.

And then she realised that she could tell Alex exactly what she was doing and he would have to listen. He couldn't talk over her, interrupt, or argue. So, each day (unless it was raining) she came and sat down beside him and told him every detail of her life without him, how she had a kitchen fitter coming to discuss the new kitchen with her, and how she was going to Corfu (yes, she had a Passport now), with her daughter for two weeks.

Now, Mary pulls herself out of the chair, folds it, packs away her flask and biscuits. 'By the way,' Mary says, 'I am going for a drink with Clive tonight. The churchwarden?' I'm not looking for another man. Not after you, but it's nice to know someone finds me interesting. I'll tell you all about it tomorrow. After all, there's nothing you can do about it now.' Mary pats the headstone and walks away.

# THE LANGUAGE OF TREES

The oak tree knows. It has stood here for hundreds of years watching over the dead. The comings and goings of mourners, the visitors who cluster or come on their own to remember, out of love or duty.

Year on year the oak has lived through the many seasons, marking the passage of time in its rings. Thicker and sturdier the trunk grows, observing, shooting branches to the light, to the heavens, roots burrowing down, fanning out.

The canopy offers shade in the heat of the summer, and backs rest against its gnarled trunk. It has stories within it that no one has sought, because people do not understand the language of trees. But it was here at the time of the flood. A first-hand account that every reporter would have sold his grandmother for. But they didn't ask.

If you listen to the trunk, put your ear against it, you will hear it breathing, liquids moving inside of it. If you listen long and hard it may tell you its history. Trees can also keep secrets.

# FEET

'I wonder why our toes aren't all the same length.'

Marjorie looks across at her daughter. 'You do ponder on some strange things.'

Pamela sits up straight in the chair and lifts one naked foot, the toenails just painted bright red and still drying. 'Maybe it's something to do with the way we walk.'

'Perhaps.' Marjorie puts down her paper. 'Maybe you should ask a chiropodist.'

'They're called podiatrists now, mum.'

'Really? I wish they wouldn't keep changing names of things, or changing how you pronounce them. So confusing.' Marjorie flips over a page in the newspaper. 'You know my mother went out with one, a chirop...pod, oh you know.'

'No, I didn't know that.'

'It was after my father walked out. Anyway, this man, the foot man, used to cycle everywhere with his black box of implements held in his hand. Should have strapped it on the back of his bike really. Much safer.'

'So, what happened?' Pamela leans forward.

'He had a foot fetish.' Marjorie shakes the paper.

'I'd have thought that went with the job.'

'Ah!' Marjorie shuts the paper and folds it. 'But his was a bit weird. He liked things done, if you know what I mean.'

'By his clients?' Pamela is now wide-eyes.

'Maybe, but certainly he asked my mother.'

'Go on.'

Marjorie sits back. 'Well, his last request ended it for her. They'd hardly dated for more than a few weeks.' She pauses. 'Liked his feet, stroked, tickled and his toes sucked.' Marjorie shudders. 'But when he asked her to whip the soles of his feet with a thin cane, well…. It's what turned him on.'

'Oh, blimey. And she did it?'

'Noooo. She showed him the door.'

'Well, I never.'

'All ended badly for him apparently.' Marjorie sniffs. 'Was found dead a few months later, his implements scattered over the floor of his flat. An erotic experiment gone wrong. Something to do with a surgical mask, Micropore and a scalpel. It was all in the newspaper. Absolute scandal. My mother was ashamed to even be linked with him.'

'I bet.'

'He's buried in that cemetery over by the river, the one that had the flood in the forties. I don't suppose there's a call for podia.. whatever there. Still, six feet under he is nearer to hell. Maybe the burning of his soles is giving him a thrill.'

# SPACE – THE FINAL FRONTIER

Justine slams her fist down on the breakfast bar. 'It's a disgrace and we can't allow this to happen.'

Dave jumps, then settles back into his Cornflakes. 'Well, I can see their quandary. There are more dead than they've places for.'

'What if it was your father?'

Dave looks up, spoon poised, milk dribbling. 'Be a miracle, would that. He'd be, what, a hundred and fifty.'

'You know what I mean.'

'You're talking ancient dead here, Justine. Look,' Dave puts his spoon in the now soggy mix. 'In London they had the same problem. Piled them high, one on top of one another.' He sees Justine shiver. 'Years later they grassed them over and made pocket parks.'

'They didn't remove them, the bodies?'

Dave shakes his head. 'Not sure. Plague victims for the most part.' Dave pushes his bowl away. Maybe he'd have toast instead.

'I was thinking of a petition. Organise a meeting in the church hall.' Justine stares at the ceiling for a second. 'After the flood, you'd have thought that enough bodies disappeared for them not to even suggest this.'

'Ah, but there's conflicting reports of that. Just how many did the cemetery lose?' Dave gets up and slips two slices of bread into the toaster. 'You should never build near a river.'

'It's not a building.'

'There's a chapel and Crem on it. Buildings, Justine. And the dead are a type of building.' He turns to Justine. 'What?' She shakes her head.

'Well, we can't have them removing old gravestones and whatever remains of those poor people.' Justine picks up the notice she's received, informing residents of the intent to re-use the oldest part of the cemetery.

'Don't think they remove them. It's called lift and deepen. Anyway, you can barely read most of the inscriptions. And some of them have sunk or are lopsided. No one visits the graves anymore.' The toaster pops up with two insipid slices. Dave takes them anyway.

The scaping of butter on toast echoes around the kitchen. Dave is so intent on this that he forgets Justine is there until, 'Well, I do.'

Dave looks up. 'Do what?'

'Visit them. And genealogists come. Why do you think the WI is logging all the graves and trying to make a map of that part of the cemetery?'

Dave lathers marmalade onto his toast. 'Are they?'

'Mary told me.' She pauses. 'I thought I might help. In fact, I was on my way, but the car won't start. Could you give me a hand?'

Dave has taken one bite of his toast. He holds it up to indicate this is breakfast time.

'You can eat that later.' Justine picks up the car keys and heads out of the door. Dave is still in his dressing gown. He shoves another mouthful of toast into his mouth and drops the rest on the plate. He follows Justine out into the damp morning. He can smell the river, and he shudders.

# DIGNITY

It takes around ninety minutes for a body to burn, and all sorts of bits and bobs get left in a coffin that shouldn't be there. They could mangle the cremator, and at £300,000 or more that's an expensive machine to repair or replace. Then there are fragments of body replacement parts – hips, knees that end up in the wheelie bin.

How long the body takes to burn is also down to how that person died. Cancer holds on to the body until the last, bugger that it is.

On the tray in the Cremulator Room the bones of the deceased now lie bleached like coral, having been fired at 850 degrees. Andrew places the bones into the tumble drier, as he calls it, and the metal balls of the machine crush the calcium into the grey ash.

In the fridge is another body waiting to be cremated. Wintertime is the busy time. The old don't cope well with cold. But it is almost summer now and not quite so frantic.

Earlier there was a Sikh family in. This is the nearest they get to a funeral pyre of India, and they witness first-hand the cremation of their loved one. Andrew struggles with that, but he knows it's their way and it means a great deal to them. It went well, but Andrew is relieved that it's over.

The process is now almost complete. The ashy remains can be placed in an urn ready for the relatives to collect, or for it to go into the ground. This one is a ground one and will take many years to rot, despite the fact that it is biodegradable.

The one in the fridge will need the big cremator. As a hefty overweight man, he won't fit into the regular one. Andrew has noticed how much more they use the bigger cremator these days. A sign of the times. Humans are a sturdy lot now, well fed, not like the poor bones of old.

He's been here for five years now, has Andrew, and he finds it strangely rewarding. He likes the fact that he and his colleagues are the last ones to take care of the deceased. They do it with dignity. Yes, there is the odd galley humour. I mean you need that now and then. He never thought he'd take to this job, but he has.

Andrew takes a break, walks out into the sunshine, lights a cigarette, raises a hand to office Harry, as he calls him. It must be lunch time because Harry is doing his usual chat with the inmates.

# ARTHUR

I hated weddings at the best of times and I really didn't want to go. The groom was Eddie's best friend and I was Eddie's plus one. But of course, Eddie was best man so I was like a spare part with no one by my side. I sat on my own in the church in my tight-fitting yellow dress like a budgie perched in a pew. Already I had begun the countdown to leaving.

Sandi, the bride, was known to me in an offhand way (she was my sister's hairdresser), but I didn't know many of Eddie's friends.

With Eddie now faffing about while the photographs were taken, I took myself off to get some peace. My feet were already killing me in my shoes. Across the road I spotted a cemetery. You couldn't get more peaceful than that. I sat down with Arthur Blackburn, 1847-1930. He'd had a good innings and he was missed by his wife, son and daughter. I wondered if I would be missed. Not when I'm dead, well, yes, when I'm dead, but more immediately, would I be missed now?

I slipped off my shoes and rested my head against Arthur's headstone. I'm sure he wouldn't mind. The sun was making me sleepy and the yellow dress was like a corset.

'Hello love.'

I looked round. 'Oh.' I began to struggle up.

'Don't get up on my account. You look right comfy there.' The elderly man raised his hat to me. He wore a dusty grey suit, tie and waistcoat.

'This dress isn't made for comfort,' I said. 'It's for wowing boyfriends.'

'Does it work?'

'Sadly not. I'm Lara, by the way, after Tomb Raider.'

The man looked baffled and I blushed realising where I was. 'Not that I'm raiding tombs.'

'Arthur.' He held out his hand.

'Oh, what a coincidence.' I took his hand. It was strangely cold on this hot day. 'I'm sitting on an Arthur's gravestone.'

'That you are.' Arthur grunted as he joined me by the gravestone.

'I'm supposed to be at a wedding over there, but no one is speaking to me.' I looked across to the milling wedding party. 'No one is going to miss me.'

'I can't believe that, a nice girl like you.'

I smiled and we sat without speaking in the heat until Arthur pulled out a pocket watch attached to a silver chain. 'Sorry love, I have to be off. Harry will be here soon.'

'Harry?'

'He works here. Always comes to say hello.'

I saw a man walking across the path in the distance. 'Is that him?' I asked, pointing. When there was no reply I turned, but Arthur had gone. Vanished. Just like that.

I struggled up and slowly made my way back to the wedding party, but I couldn't get Arthur out of my head.

# RADIATION

The ground is as hard as the bones underneath it. In the hot breeze, yellowing grass has gone to stubble or seed. If the dead are ever restless this would be their time. Under foot, the ground cracks for want of water and even the river has lost the energy to produce more than a trickle. Summer is caught in a heat haze and mirages flutter above the graves. You could be forgiven for the thinking these were outlines of the departed, braving the daylight hours just for a whiff of nostalgia, before bedding down once more in the cool earth.

Visitors come in the early morning or late afternoon to avoid the worst of the heat. Mary comes with breakfast boxed up in Tupperware to sit beside Alex, before joining the WI to carry on with their plotting of the older graves. They are joined by Justine, a new recruit, dressed in pristine white shorts and a purpose.

Harry has flung the office windows wide. The fan whirls on its fastest speed while papers are held down with staplers, a coffee mug and a hole puncher. He glances outside at the shimmering headstones, sees Joe watering the rose bed, though his eyes are staring at the woman in the white shorts.

And Harry notices that smell again and wonders if it is the drains. The putrid aroma rises every so often like a rotting corpse. Harry shakes his head. He's worked here too long.

Outside, stonework absorbs the heat, gathering every ounce of radiation for later, a sort of solar storage heater for the relics to cling on to.

# SIXTH SENSE

Leaves tumble in golden swirls. The sun lies low, tips the falling leaves with radiant light. Reds, yellows, greens, browns, shower down on Angela as she walks Bimbo, her long haired dachshund. Under her feet, the crisp carpet of autumnal colours crunch. Bimbo noses in and out of the undergrowth looking for whatever dogs look for.

Angela read the cards this morning and her mind is troubled. Something's coming. Something worrying, but she tries to walk off the feeling and takes the path down to the river. When she reaches where the cemetery railings begin, her feet squelch in mud. The river has swollen since the recent rains, and the sound of it rushing is normally calming music to Angela, but today the bankside is saturated. Through the railings there are puddles close to the ancient graves. She trudges on remembering the stories she's heard.

Coming to the little footbridge, Angela begins to cross it, away from the town. Half way she stops and looks down into the swirling water, while Bimbo sniffs around before cocking his leg against the wall. Angela's head feels woozy. The smell of the river fills her nostrils. Something putrid and cloying makes Angela cough and wretch. A second later the smell had vanished.

The river has spoken. There is a warning in there, just like in the cards.

# THE WRONG MAN

'I hope that doesn't come back to haunt us,' Reverend Steve Phillips says, frowning into his pint at *The Swan*.

His curate Tom smiles. 'You couldn't write that stuff.'

'It's not funny. This could land us in serious trouble.' Steve takes a swig of his pint and raises his eyes to heaven. 'And why did no one say anything? That's what I don't understand.'

'Well, they did.'

'Yes, afterwards. Afterwards Tom, not during. Not when I was reading the eulogy with all the wrong names and all the wrong facts.'

Tom puts a hand on the vicar's arm. 'There were only two people there. They couldn't have known him well.'

'Well enough. Well, they thought they did until I gave them a version of Reginald's life they never knew existed. Jesus!' Reverend Steve puts a hand to his head, stares at the optics behind the bar.

'It's not your fault,' Tom says.

'Of course it's my fault! It's my job not to get the deceased mixed up, not to commit the wrong body to the ground. No wonder the undertakers gave me a funny look.' Steve's eyes are glassy. 'It wasn't until that man came up afterwards and said, *I always thought he was called Edward* that I realised something was wrong.'

'Yes, I know…'

'And then he said, *I never knew he did all those things*.'

'Yes, but…'

'If only Father Timothy hadn't fallen ill. If only he'd asked someone else to take the two funerals. Now I've got to go and take the same service over the right man.'

'I can see that…' but Tom stops.

'What?'

'That man over there. Isn't he…?'

Reverend Steve turns. 'Oh Lord save me! Let's go.' The two abandon their drinks and try to sneak out. But two men wearing dog collars kind of stand out in a pub.

'Hey, vicar!' The man in the corner calls. The two men of God stop. 'I was just telling these guys about Edward or Reginald, whatever he liked to call himself. What a man! Will you join us?'

'Sadly, we can't,' says Reverend Steve.

'We have another funeral to…' Steve stands on Tom's foot. 'Ow,' Tom yells.

'Must go,' Steve says.

Outside Tom says, 'I don't remember there being a clause in my contract about the right of your vicar to stamp on his curate's foot whenever it so pleases him.'

'I'm in pain, Tom. I don't want to bear it alone.'

'But the Almighty shares your pain with you, Steve.'

'Yes, but I don't suppose our Creator ever got people mixed up. After all, he said, 'I have summoned you by name; you are mine' Isaiah 43:1'

'Well, there is that,' Tom agrees, and they walk silently away from the pub back to the cemetery.

# RIVER RISING

The rain began one November morning and would not stop. For days the town was drenched in sheets of it. On the third day a wind got up. The chimney of Mrs Hardy's house crashed down and garden furniture romped across lawns, over fences, and one white plastic patio table was seen floating down river towards the lock, where a blockage was building up. The Environment Agency kicked into action. Defences were put in place and the patio table was removed.

The little footbridge had stood for centuries and had been due for repairs for the last five years. The local council had pleaded lack of money. 'Our hands are tied,' they said. 'Blame central government,' the local Labour MP said. 'They hold the purse strings.' And all the while the footbridge held together.

A hundred metres down was the road bridge. Sturdy and well built, it could hold its own against the rising water. But the river was angry and whipped by the wind it had nowhere to go except into fields and roads. By the end of the week a crack had appeared on the bridge and it was too dangerous to cross.

The little footbridge was now the only means of crossing over from one side of the river to the other. But soon bits began to drop off it. Bricks and mortar washed away on the swell down river.

At the cemetery there were fears of a 1948 repeat, as river water sloshed over the banks and seeped into the lower edge.

At the time a small funeral was taking place. Enoch Bannister from the other side of the river was about to be buried in the saturated earth. A few mourners braved the rain, but the affair was most notable for the young man standing in handcuffs and guarded by prison officers. White faced and with a bowed head he watched as his father was laid to rest with his mother.

A worried Harry from the cemetery office watched as water crept evermore near. Would the sandbags be enough or should they abandon the office while they could?

Down in the old part of the cemetery Justine was wringing her hands. All her hard work with petitions and meetings against the re-using of ancient graves would be for nothing if this section was flooded.

The oak tree watched on and passed the information to the surrounding trees, as some of its weaker limbs snapped away from the trunk. Then as suddenly as the rain had begun, it stopped. The clouds parted and the sun laid its golden head across the cemetery like a saving angel. A collective sigh could almost be heard by the living and dead. The water would recede and everything would be safe for now, maybe for years to come. The dead could gather once more to tell their stories, if that was indeed what they did.

# ACKNOWLEDGEMENT

My grateful thanks to Diane Fraser-Watson who has been my encourager, beta reader and proof-reader throughout every stage of bringing this book to publication. Your comments, suggestions and help have been invaluable. To my friends at London Free-Writing Meetup, thanks for the opportunity to participate in such a lively and fun group.

# ABOUT THE AUTHOR

## Heather Walker

Heather Walker writes poetry and short fiction. She has been published online and in print, including Paragraph Planet, Visual Verse, OU Poets, Gold Dust, What the Dickens? and The People's Friend. Her work has also appeared in several anthologies, including What Was Left (Retreat West), Light Through the Mist (Helen Cox Books) and Eyelands. She once had a poem displayed alongside art works in The Artist Rifles exhibition in Basingstoke. She lives in London.

Twitter: @heather91404743

Website: storyandverse.blogspot.com

# AFTERWORD

I hope you have enjoyed this little book.

Please do leave a review on Amazon. Authors are very interested to learn what readers think.

Thanks.

Printed in Great Britain
by Amazon